SADIQ

and the
Fun Run

BY **SIMAN NUURALI**

ART BY **ANJAN SARKAR**

Raintree is an imprint of Capstone Global Library Limited, a company
incorporated in England and Wales having its registered office at
264 Banbury Road, Oxford, OX2 7DY – Registered company number:
6695582

www.raintree.co.uk
myorders@raintree.co.uk

Design by Brann Garvey
Design Element: Shutterstock/Irtsya
Original illustrations by Anjan Sarkar
Original illustrations © Capstone Global Library Limited 2020
Originated by Capstone Global Library Ltd
Printed and bound in India

ISBN 978 1 4747 7210 5
23 22 21 20 19
10 9 8 7 6 5 4 3 2 1

British Library Catal
A full catalogue recor

CONTENTS

FACTS ABOUT SOMALIA

- Most Somali people belong to one of four major groups: the Darod, Isaaq, Hawiye and Dir.
- Many Somalis in Africa are nomadic. That means they travel from place to place. They search for water, food and land for their animals.
- Somalia is mostly desert. It doesn't rain often there.
- The camel is an important animal to Somali people. Camels can survive a long time without food or water.
- Around ninety-nine per cent of all Somalis are Muslim.

SOMALI TERMS

baba (BAH-baah) common word for father

cambuulo (UHM-boo-loh) dish made up of rice and beans, with sesame oil and sugar drizzled on top

hooyo (HOY-yoh) mother

salaam (sa-LAHM) short form of Arabic greeting, used by many Muslims. It also means "peace".

wiilkeyga (wil-KAY-gaah) my son

CHAPTER 1

AMERICAN FOOTBALL TRIALS

On Sunday afternoon, Sadiq went to the park near his house. Leaves crunched under his feet as he walked. He spotted Zaza and Manny tossing a ball back and forth.

"Sadiq!" called Zaza. "Have you heard about the new school American football team? We're going to the trials."

Manny threw the football to Sadiq as he walked closer. "Are you guys both going to try it?" asked Sadiq.

"I am," replied Zaza. "Both of my older brothers play American football. It looks like so much fun."

"Me too!" said Manny. "I hope I get on the team. The uniforms are so cool!"

"Are you going to give it a go, Sadiq?" asked Zaza.

"I would like to, but I'll have to ask my parents first," said Sadiq.

The boys continued to pass the ball to each other. They practised snapping the ball. They practised short throws and long throws. And finally, they practised catching the ball while running. *Zaza and Manny are really good!* Sadiq thought. *Maybe if I practise enough I'll be just as good.*

When it started to get dark outside, Sadiq headed home. He went to look for his mum straight away. He wanted to talk to her about joining the team. Zaza and Manny had made it sound so exciting!

"*Salaam*, *Hooyo*!" Sadiq called as he pushed through the front door. It smelled of *cambuulo*, a bean dish made with butter and sugar. It was one of Sadiq's favourite meals, and he was hungry!

"Salaam, Sadiq," Hooyo said. She looked up from a magazine she was reading while dinner cooked on the hob beside her. "How was the park?"

"Good! Zaza, Manny and I played American football," Sadiq explained. "Trials for the team are tomorrow. Is *Baba* home? I wanted to ask you both if I could join."

"Aren't you all too young to play American football?" said Hooyo. She looked a little worried.

"What's this about American football?" Baba asked as he walked into the kitchen.

"Pull up a chair for your baba and set the table, please," Hooyo said as she passed some plates and utensils to Sadiq.

"I want to join the school team," Sadiq said.

"I don't think that's a good idea. You're only eight, *wiilkeyga*," Baba said, sitting down. "Your brother didn't start playing until he was twelve."

"I agree," said Hooyo. She pulled some napkins out of a drawer and handed them to Sadiq.

Sadiq went around the table and put a napkin at each place setting as he complained. "But Zaza and Manny are going to! Their parents don't think they're too young."

"That may be true, wiilkeyga, but it can be a very rough game. I don't want you to get hurt," said Baba.

"I would be very worried too," said Hooyo. "I think you should wait until you're older, like your brother."

Sadiq looked down at the floor, disappointed.

"I know you're sad, Sadiq, but is there another club you can join at school? Something other than American football?" asked Hooyo.

Sadiq shook his head sadly. "I want to be on a team with Manny and Zaza."

Baba spoke up. "We got your school newsletter the other day. There's going to be a running club starting later this week, and anyone can join in! Ahmed Bilaal is coaching it."

"Is he the runner who qualified for the national team?" asked Hooyo.

"Yes!" said Baba. "A famous runner will be coaching at your school, Sadiq."

"But what about my friends? Zaza and Manny are going to have so much fun without me," Sadiq said, sadly.

"They'll still be your friends, wiilkeyga," Hooyo said. "Maybe you can take them running with you."

Just then, Sadiq's brother, Nuurali, wandered into the room. "Running will help you get better at football," he said. "It helps me stay in shape. That's why I run a few times a week."

Sadiq perked up. He was still disappointed about American football, but he did *love* ordinary football. "I guess I can give it a try," he said.

* * *

"My parents won't let me try out for American football," said Sadiq as he, Zaza and Manny waited for the bus to pick them up on Monday morning.

"Why not?" Manny said.

"They think I'm too young. Nuurali didn't start playing until he was twelve," Sadiq explained.

"Did you tell them that we're both doing it?" asked Zaza. He sounded very disappointed.

Sadiq nodded. "They want me to try the Running Club instead."

"Running?!" Manny said. "Running is so boring."

"I hoped we'd all be on the team together," said Zaza.

"I know," said Sadiq as the bus pulled up. "Me too."

CHAPTER 2

SUPER RACER

After school on Tuesday, Sadiq walked to the bus alone. He felt sorry for himself. Manny and Zaza had made the American football team. They'd found out at lunchtime, and today was their first practice.

As he walked past the football pitch, Sadiq could see his friends warming up. He felt left out. Manny and Zaza looked really tough in all their new gear.

As Sadiq watched, a player wearing a blue jersey ran with the ball. Players wearing yellow jerseys chased him down the field. They caught up and tackled him! The player who had been running with the ball got up and dusted himself off. He jogged back to his teammates.

I don't understand why Baba and Hooyo won't let me play football, Sadiq thought. *I could become strong like that player. It would be so much fun to tackle people!*

When Sadiq got home, he was not in a good mood. He was upset after seeing how much fun Zaza, Manny and all the other kids were having.

He went straight to his room, where he found Nuurali doing homework on the computer they shared for schoolwork.

Sadiq threw his rucksack on the floor and flopped face down on his bed.

"What's the matter, Sadiq?" asked Nuurali. "Are you all right?"

"No!" said Sadiq, his voice muffled in his pillow. He looked up. "I saw Zaza and Manny playing American football. They were having all the fun in the world! It's not fair that Baba and Hooyo won't let me play."

"Well, you could have fun in your Running Club pretty soon," said Nuurali. "Don't you start practice tomorrow?"

"Yes, practice starts tomorrow. But I'd rather be at American football practice," said Sadiq as he sat up and faced his brother.

"You won't know until you try," said Nuurali. "I could do with a break from my homework. Would you like to come running with me? It might help you get ready for your first practice."

"No," said Sadiq, sulking.

"Come on, Sadiq," Nuurali said. "I don't want to run alone!"

"Fine," said Sadiq. He got up and dragged himself to the wardrobe to find his sports clothes and trainers.

After Nuurali and Sadiq got changed, they met up by the front door.

"My football coach says to always start with a slow jog. It helps you save energy so you don't get tired straight away," Nuurali said as he tied his shoelaces.

They went outside and started running down the road.

"You have to loosen your arms and keep them close to your body," said Nuurali.

After a few minutes, Sadiq started to feel hot and thirsty. "I don't really want to jog any more, Nuurali," he said.

"We've only just started, Sadiq," said Nuurali. "Let's at least get to the end of the corner."

"But it's so far away," said Sadiq, slowing to a walk.

"Come on, Sadiq!" Nuurali called over his shoulder. "Breathe in and out. Before you know it, we'll be home!"

"I didn't want to go in the first place," said Sadiq. "I only came because you asked."

Nuurali slowed down so he could walk with Sadiq.

"You know, Sadiq," Nuurali said, "if you get really good at running you might even be able to compete in track and field or cross country when you're older."

Sadiq was now dragging his feet along the pavement.

"Running will also help you get better at other sports like football," said Nuurali, smiling.

"I guess so," said Sadiq. He kicked a rock down the pavement.

"Come on, Super Racer!" Nuurali called. "Last one home does the dishes tonight!" He laughed as he started running again.

Sadiq sighed and ran after his brother.

CHAPTER 3

RUNNING CLUB

The next day, Sadiq went to the track after school. It was time for the first Running Club practice, and Sadiq was nervous. Running with Nuurali had been hard. *What if I'm not any good at running?* Sadiq thought. A young man wearing a tracksuit and holding a clipboard was already on the track when Sadiq arrived. There were several kids surrounding him.

"Hello there!" the man said. "I'm Ahmed. I'll be your running coach." He held out his hand to Sadiq.

"I'm Sadiq." Sadiq shook Ahmed's hand.

When everyone had arrived, Ahmed told them, "The Running Club will meet after school for practice each day. Towards the end of the season, we'll all run in a 5K Fun Run. We will need to train properly so we don't get too tired or sore."

Next they went round the circle for introductions. Sadiq knew a couple of the kids who were in his year. He had never met some of the others.

When they were done, Ahmed asked if they had any questions.

"Is it true you've won medals?" asked a boy named Hafid. "You must be fast."

Ahmed laughed. "I have won medals in some races," he said. "And I still hold the regional junior record for the 1500 metre track race."

"Wow!" said Sadiq.

"Was it hard training to compete?" asked Grace.

"It was," said Ahmed. "I used to wake up every morning at five. I would run for an hour before school. Sometimes I wanted to give up. But my baba encouraged me to keep training."

Five o'clock?! Sadiq thought. *It must take a lot of hard work to become such a fast runner.*

Next it was time to warm up. The team did jumping jacks and stretches.

"Bend over as far as you can and touch your toes," said Ahmed, leading them through some stretches. "You should have a slight bend in your knees."

"That's easy!" said Hafid.

But when Hafid tried to do it, he couldn't touch his toes. He lost his balance and fell forwards onto the track! "It's harder than I thought," he said, laughing.

After stretching, Ahmed explained their workout. "I would like you all to take two laps around the track. Jog at a pace that's comfortable for you."

They all took off.

A tall girl named Hayla ran beside Sadiq. "Hi!" she said, smiling. "My dad says I have long legs and that's good for running."

"I'm not very tall. I don't know if that's good or bad for running," said Sadiq, smiling back.

After one lap, Hafid piped up. "Let's race!"

Hafid, Hayla and Sadiq all sprinted ahead of the group.

Soon they crossed the finish line, followed by the rest of the team. They were all breathing hard.

"So, team, how do you feel?" asked Ahmed.

"Ver–very tired. I didn't . . . thin–
think it was this . . . hard," said Sadiq,
out of breath.

"I'm exhausted," said Hayla.

"That was a good start," Ahmed
said. "But at our first practice, you
shouldn't be sprinting. You have to
learn to pace yourself. Can anyone tell
me what *pace* means?"

"It means to go at a steady speed – not too fast or too slow," said a girl named Kianna.

"Right!" said Ahmed. "You want to make sure you can keep your pace for the whole time you're running. It will get easier as the season goes on."

"I don't . . . think so . . . ," said Hafid, still breathing hard.

Ahmed laughed. "I promise, the first day is the hardest."

Everyone was silent except for the huffing and puffing.

"Let's all jog in place for a few minutes to let our heart rates slow down," said Ahmed. "It will help us breathe better and help us recover."

The kids did as they were told. After a few minutes Ahmed asked them to stop and have a drink.

"Does anyone have any questions?" asked Ahmed, as everyone got their water bottles.

"How far are we going to run at practice?" a boy named Matt asked.

"Good question, Matt," said Ahmed. "It will be different every practice, but the most we will run is five kilometres. The Fun Run we'll participate in at the end of the season is also five kilometres."

"The most I've ever run is one-and-a-half kilometres!" said Grace. "That was for football practice."

"If you play football, I bet you've run more than that!" said Ahmed. "Most football players run a few kilometres during a game."

Sadiq was surprised by that. "I play football," he said excitedly to Hayla and Hafid. "I bet I can run five kilometres!"

"Me too," Hafid said.

"Next time let's work on our pace. Then we won't get so tired," said Hayla.

"Good work today, team!" said Ahmed. "Practice is over. I'll see you tomorrow."

CHAPTER 4

LEFT OUT

"How is American football practice going?" Sadiq asked Zaza and Manny at lunch on Thursday.

"It's *awesome*!" said Manny, grinning.

"I wish you had been there yesterday to see our first scrimmage!" Zaza said. He took a sip of his juice. "Manny and I were on the same team. We were down by three points with only a minute left. The whole team was on their feet cheering."

"Our quarterback, Jack, threw the ball way down the field to Eric," said Manny. "He was so far away we thought the ball would go out of bounds."

"But Eric jumped up really high and caught the ball," said Manny.

"He ran faster than I have ever seen anyone run and then . . . TOUCHDOWN!" said Zaza.

Sadiq nodded and said, "Cool," but he was feeling very left out. Zaza and Manny hadn't asked him anything about Running Club.

After a minute or two of silence, Sadiq spoke up. "Running Club is also pretty cool. Our coach is a famous athlete."

"What did you do at practice?" Zaza asked.

"We did stretching exercises and then ran a couple of laps," said Sadiq.

"Is that all?" said Zaza. He laughed, looking at Manny.

"That doesn't sound too hard," said Manny.

"It was actually kind of difficult," Sadiq said quietly.

Why are they being so rude? Sadiq wondered. *Running is just as tough as American football.*

Embarrassed, he packed up the rest of his lunch and went back to class early.

* * *

That afternoon at Running Club practice, Sadiq couldn't stop thinking about what Manny and Zaza had said. He felt annoyed and embarrassed that his friends didn't think running was a tough sport. Distracted, Sadiq slowed to a walk.

"What's wrong, buddy?" asked Ahmed, jogging up next to him.

"Nothing," said Sadiq. He didn't really want to talk about it.

"You can talk to me if something's bothering you, Sadiq," said Ahmed. "I know that being unhappy can really affect your running."

"My friends bragged about how tough American football is," said Sadiq. "It made me think running isn't as tough."

"In order to be a good American football player, you have to be a really good runner as well."

"That's true," said Sadiq. That made him feel a little better.

"When I was a boy, I wanted to become a fast runner but I didn't want to train. Then one day at practice I stepped in a hole and twisted my ankle," said Ahmed.

"Ouch!" said Sadiq.

"I went from not wanting to run to not being able to walk very well. I had to use crutches for a couple of weeks and watch as my teammates competed," Ahmed explained.

"That doesn't sound fun," said Sadiq.

"It wasn't," said Ahmed. "But sitting out while the others had fun and improved made me appreciate running!"

Sadiq thought about that. If he wasn't able to run, he'd be sad too!

"From that day on," Ahmed said, "I was determined to practise as much as I could. Running became more fun. That is how I became a good runner."

"I'm sorry I wasn't trying today," said Sadiq. "I promise to try hard from now on."

"That's great," said Ahmed. "High five?" He held out his hand.

"High five!" said Sadiq. He slapped Ahmed's hand in return.

CHAPTER 5

THE FUN RUN

For the next few weeks, Sadiq worked very hard with the rest of his team. He was getting much better. Sadiq could run many laps without stopping or slowing down! He was starting to like running, but he still missed his friends.

Manny and Zaza had tried to talk to him a few times, but Sadiq was still upset by what they'd said to him about running. He didn't want to hang out with his friends if they gave him a hard time about running being an easy sport.

"Okay, team," Ahmed said after practice one day. "Next weekend is the Fun Run. Remember – it's not just about winning. But I want everyone to try their very best and finish feeling proud."

"Do you have any advice for us, Coach?" asked Hayla.

"It's a good idea to team up and run together in groups," said Ahmed. "That way you can push each other on when one of you gets tired."

"Want to run together?" Hafid whispered to Hayla and Sadiq.

The trio nodded and smiled at one another.

* * *

Finally it was time for the Fun Run! Sadiq was very excited, but he was also nervous. His family drove him to the course, then went to find a spot to watch. There were lots of kids around, all in running gear! It took Sadiq a few minutes to spot his running team.

"Hi, you guys!" Sadiq called to them.

"Hi, Sadiq!" they all replied, waving at him.

"Gather round, kids. I have a surprise for you!" said Ahmed.

"What is it?" asked Hafid.

Ahmed leaned down and opened a box. He took out . . . UNIFORMS! They were silver, with all the kids' names printed in purple on the back.

"Look how cool they are!" said Sadiq.

"I love this lightning bolt on the front side," said Hayla.

"That's because we are fast like lightning!" said Hafid, laughing.

* * *

Soon it was time for the race. Ahmed gave the team a pep talk. "Remember to stay focused and try your best," he said. "And team up!"

Sadiq and his friends jogged over to the starting line and waited for the signal.

"Ready . . . set . . . go!" the starter yelled.

Sadiq, Hafid and Hayla teamed up and took the lead straight away. A few other runners ran just behind them. Sadiq set the pace, and Hafid and Hayla ran a step behind him. Soon they had finished one mile!

They were running too hard to say much to each other. Their pace was fast, but Sadiq felt like he could keep going.

Hafid kept pushing himself, but halfway through the second mile, he started to fade.

"I don't think I can keep up," said Hafid. He looked tired. "You should go ahead."

Sadiq could see Hayla was also falling behind, but he didn't want to leave his friends.

"I'll run with Hafid," said Hayla as they completed the second mile.

"Are you sure?" asked Sadiq.

"Yes," said Hayla. "We'll be right behind you."

"Okay, good luck!" Sadiq said as he took off. Sadiq pushed himself and ran faster than he had ever run before.

Running had seemed easier with Hayla and Hafid. He started to feel really tired.

Sadiq looked up to see how far he was from the finish line. Just then he spotted two familiar faces in the crowd.

Zaza and Manny! They had come to watch him race! *But how did they find out about the race?* Sadiq wondered.

He ran even harder, wanting to impress them. He wanted to show everyone how hard he had been working at practice. He pushed himself harder and harder until he crossed the finish line.

Sadiq had won!

His family ran down from the stands to congratulate him. Baba lifted him up in the air!

"Good job, Sadiq!" said Baba. "That was a really great run!"

Just then, Ahmed jogged over and gave Sadiq a high five.

"How did you run so fast?" asked Hooyo.

"I don't know!" said Sadiq. He was still breathing hard.

"He trained really well and worked very hard," replied Ahmed.

"We're very proud of you, Sadiq," Hooyo said.

Soon Hayla and Hafid crossed the finish line together. They had tied for second place! Before Sadiq could make it over to congratulate them, Zaza and Manny ran over to him. "Hi, champ!" said Zaza, hugging Sadiq.

"Hi, guys!" Sadiq said. He high-fived Manny. "How did you know my race was today?"

"We saw a sign at school," Manny said. "I can't believe how fast you ran!"

"So you don't think running is for wimps after all?" Sadiq asked. "You really hurt my feelings when you said that."

"We're really sorry we said running seemed easy," said Manny.

"We didn't mean to make you feel bad," said Zaza. "And it seems like running is really tough."

"It's okay. But you're right. Running *is* hard," said Sadiq.

"So what do you think, Sadiq?" asked Ahmed. "Will you stay in Running Club?"

"Yes!" Sadiq said. He turned to Zaza and Manny. "Do you want to come to Running Club sometime?" he asked.

"Can we?" asked Zaza excitedly, looking up at Ahmed.

"Of course you can," replied Ahmed. "We have one more practice this season. It's on Monday after school. Everyone is welcome."

"Football season is over now. Maybe we can come with you!" said Manny.

"I hope I'm not still tired from the race by then," said Sadiq.

Everyone laughed.

GLOSSARY

affect influence or change someone or something

appreciate enjoy or value somebody or something

champ short for *champion*; the winner of a competition

compete try hard to outdo others at a task, race or contest

congratulate offer good wishes to someone when something good has happened

impress make someone feel admiration or respect

introduction presentation of one person to another

muffled when a sound is quieter or less clear

newsletter short written report that tells the recent news of an organization

pace rate of speed, or to move at a certain speed

qualified became eligible for a competition by reaching a certain standard

quarterback in American football, the player who leads the attack by throwing the ball or handing it to a runner

recover return to a normal state of health or strength

scrimmage in American football, a practice game between two teams

tackle knock or throw a player to the ground in order to stop a player from moving forward

touchdown in American football, a play in which the ball is carried over the opponent's goal line, scoring six points

wimp weak person

TALK ABOUT IT

1. What reasons did Sadiq's parents give for not letting him try American football? Do you think they were being fair?

2. Sadiq feels left out when his friends Manny and Zaza talk about their American football team. Share an experience you've had of feeling left out.

3. Sadiq receives a lot of encouragement as he trains for the Fun Run. Who helps Sadiq prepare? Discuss how they help him.

WRITE IT DOWN

1. Write an article for Sadiq's school newsletter about the Fun Run. You can interview Sadiq and others in the Running Club for your story.

2. Ahmed is famous for his running ability. Have you ever met someone famous? If so, write a paragraph explaining your experience. If not, write a paragraph about a famous person you would love to meet.

3. At first, running is not so easy for Sadiq. Have you ever tried something that was difficult at first? Write a paragraph about your experience.

HOME WORKOUT!

Sadiq learns to improve his fitness when he joins the Running Club. With this short home workout, you can too! Make sure to pace yourself and take breaks for a drink if you get tired. This workout can also be done with a partner.

WHAT YOU NEED:

- space to move around
- clothes suitable for exercise
- tape
- water

WHAT TO DO:

1. Find a space in your home where you'll have plenty of room to move around in.

2. Place a line of tape in your workout area. This will be used for one of the exercises.

3. Start your workout with stretches. It's important for your muscles to be stretched before any workout!

4. Do ten sit-ups. You may need a partner to help keep your feet on the ground.

5. Now complete ten push-ups.

6. Do fifteen jumping jacks.

7. Try to jump back and forth over the line of tape fifteen times.

8. Repeat the workout until you feel like you need a break. See if you can increase your numbers of sit-ups, push-ups, jumping jacks and tape-line jumps the more times you do the workout.

9. Make sure you drink water after your workout.

CREATORS

Siman Nuurali grew up in Kenya. She now lives in Minnesota, USA. Siman and her family are Somali – just like Sadiq and his family! She and her five children love to play badminton and board games together. Siman works at the Children's Hospital and, in her free time, she also enjoys writing and reading.

Anjan Sarkar is a British illustrator based in Sheffield. Since he was little, Anjan has always loved drawing stuff. And now he gets to draw stuff all day for his job. Hooray! In addition to the Sadiq series, Anjan has been drawing mischievous kids, undercover aliens and majestic tigers for other exciting children's book projects.